GRANDMA'S GENERAL STORE
THE ARK

DOROTHY CARTER

PICTURES BY THOMAS B. ALLEN

GRANDMA'S
GENERAL STORE
·THE ARK·

FRANCES FOSTER BOOKS

FARRAR, STRAUS and GIROUX • NEW YORK

www.fsgkidsbooks.com

Library of Congress Cataloging-in-Publication Data
Carter, Dorothy (Dorothy A.)
     Grandma's general store : the Ark / Dorothy Carter ; pictures by
Thomas B. Allen.— 1st ed.
        p. cm.
     Summary: In the 1930s when their parents go north to
Philadelphia to find work, five-year-old Pearl and seven-year-old
Prince must stay behind with their grandmother in Florida and help
her run her small store.
     ISBN-13: 978-0-374-32766-8
     ISBN-10: 0-374-32766-1
     1. African Americans—Juvenile fiction.   [1. African Americans—
Fiction.   2. Grandmothers—Fiction.   3. Brothers and sisters—
Fiction.   4. Florida—Race relations—Fiction.]   I. Allen, Thomas B.,
ill.   II. Title.

PZ7.C2433 Gr 2005
[Fic]—dc21

                                                    2002026591

To wise and caring grandmothers—then and now
—D.C.

To Tom Feelings
—T.A.

CONTENTS

GRANDMA'S GENERAL STORE
THE ARK

that Grandma had won at the church bazaar hung above the bench. It showed a woman sweeping her yard and words beneath saying, "If each before her own door sweep, the village would be clean." Me and Prince memorized those words and repeated them by heart. "We can read. We can read," we bragged.

But today, the people kept on laughing and talking. They didn't look at me and Prince. We wanted them to notice us, so we stood in the middle of the store and made faces till Grandma shook her finger at us. She meant for us to stop showing off. Then Reverend Hill stood up and faced the picture. He pointed to every other word, like "sweep," "village," "clean," and we pronounced them. He was testing us, but that was easy. We knew how to match the name with its shape.

The customers clapped their hands and said, "That's mighty fine, mighty fine, children." Then they went right back to their talk.

After that, Grandma told us to feed the chickens.

The chicken feed was near the case. It was stuffed with Fig Newtons, banana caramels, jaw-

GRANDMA'S GENERAL STORE
THE ARK

"Race you, Pearl. The last one to Grandma's is a rotten egg," Prince dared me.

"The first one there is a polecat," I came back at him. I could run as fast as Prince, though he was almost seven and I was still five.

We raced to the store, just next door to the house where me and Prince lived with Mama and Daddy. Me and Prince had two homes where we played, ate, and slept whenever we wanted.

Grandma called the store an "add-on." Grandpa built it onto their ready-made house. "It's my Ark," she said.

"What's an Ark?" I asked.

Grandma paused a long while before she answered. "A shelter from the storms of life. It keeps you from being tossed away."

"Grandma, are you scared of storms?"

"No, child. Only the ones I don't expect. They make a heap of trouble and pain." Grandma talked riddles at times.

The store sat on a ridge above the railroad tracks. Every day we waved at the train chugging along, blowing its whistle and spitting out steam. It smelled hot and smoky. "Stay away from that railroad crossing," Grandma warned.

Watching the colored customers and white merchants straggle into the store was our favorite thing to do. They talked a lot and we listened. Grandma was always saying, "They're just here to palaver."

When I asked her what "palaver" meant, she said, "Business is slow for the merchants, and my customers don't have much money to spend. They're just here waiting around and treating themselves to a cold soda and a sweet snack to help pass the time of day. We laugh and talk together."

The customers squeezed together on a bench facing the counter where Grandma kept the scales and charging ledger. A framed picture

breakers, Baby Ruths, Snickers, licorice, and every other kind of candy there was. We put a pile of cookies and candy on top of the bowl of chicken feed.

Grandma shouted, "Stay out of that case. You're gonna make yourself sick, and you're eating up my profit."

After we fed and watered the chickens, we ran home to see what Mama and Daddy were doing.

"What you two young'uns been up to?" Daddy asked as he tickled us. Daddy and Prince played boxing. "I'm Jack Johnson," said Prince.

"Okay, Mr. Heavyweight Champion of the World, hit me if you can." Prince couldn't reach high enough to hit Daddy.

"Let me ride on your back, Daddy," I asked.

Prince kept hopping around and punching Daddy. I punched and pulled Daddy, and we all screamed and laughed. Daddy dropped to his knees so I could climb on his back. He jumped up and trotted around the room, saying, "Ride 'em, cowgirl!"

Mama yelled, "Hush your noisy mouths and

help me fold your clean clothes and put them in the drawers. I can't think straight in all this confusion your daddy and you young'uns are making!"

We raced right back to Grandma's store.

THE SKY IS FALLING

With Grandma's store and our house we had a kingdom!

Nothing ever bothered us until that time we came home and saw Mama sobbing and trembling and walking back and forth between the kitchen and the front porch.

"Why you crying, Mama?" I asked.

"Are you sick, Mama?" asked Prince.

"I'm not sick. Your daddy's not home. It's getting late."

The sun had gone down. Most working people were home doing little patch-up jobs. When Daddy came home from work, he always washed the lamp shades, hauled in buckets of water, and filled the oil-stove tank with kerosene. During warm weather Mama cooked on her oil stove to keep down the heat.

"It's way past time for Daddy to be home." Prince was looking at the clock. He could tell time.

"Pearl, go see if your daddy is coming down the road," Mama said.

The light at the railroad crossing was blinking.

"I don't see him, Mama. The road is too dark . . ."

"Where on earth is that man?" Mama came and stood in the middle of the road. She looked in every direction. "Don't let him be there. Please, not there," Mama mumbled.

"I'm gonna get Grandma!" I leaped next door to Grandma's house.

"Daddy ain't home yet!" I shouted as I entered Grandma's kitchen. "Mama don't know where he is! She's scared and she's crying."

"Go tell your Mama I'm coming! Something is wrong!" Grandma said.

Grandma slid the bar across the front door of the store and lit the lamp. I ran back home, with Grandma right behind me. Mama threw her apron on the swing and unpinned her hair.

Grandma and Mama walked fast, but me and Prince kept up with them.

I whispered, "Do you think Daddy has gone to Eternity where Grandpa lives?"

"Naw, Pearl. Daddy is no sick old man like Grandpa was," Prince said.

"Mercy, Lord, mercy, mercy!" Mama kept on saying that.

"Stop crying, Mama! We're helping you find Daddy. Maybe he's making a joke," Prince said. He took Mama's hand.

"Ruth, I'm scared he's lapsed," said Grandma.

"Mama, don't badmouth Joe!"

"There's Tom Johnson coming our way," said Grandma.

Mr. Tom Johnson worked at the sawmill with our daddy. He tipped his hat to Mama and Grandma. "How y'all fine ladies doing this evening?"

"Tom, we're glad to see you. We're looking for Joe. Have you seen him?" Mama asked.

"Not since he was arguing with Mr. Moss 'bout losing his job as the mill foreman."

"He lost his job at the sawmill?" Mama said.

"Mr. Moss told him he had to lay him off and put young Ben Moss in charge of running the mill. Said his son needs to learn the business. Said he was worn out. Mr. Moss owns the mill and he can do what he wants," Mr. Tom explained. "Joe lost his temper and talked back in Mr. Moss's face, acting like he owned the mill. Y'all know for a fact, Joe is one uppity, ornery po' colored man trying to act like he's a white man. People say y'all are color struck. Wanna be white."

"Tom is the right name for you," Grandma muttered. "Still Uncle Tomming and toadying up to the boss man! Trying to get on the good side of Mr. Moss."

The moon and stars were hidden far up in the sky. It was pitch-dark all around us. We stumbled over the ruts in the road and stepped in mud puddles. We held on to each other to keep from falling.

Mama said, "Maybe he stopped into town to buy us some fresh meat from the Piggly Wiggly."

Grandma said, "More likely, he stopped at the moonshine 'stillery."

We didn't know where to go. "It's too dark and dangerous for us to be out here," said Grandma.

We ran home. Prince held on to Mama's hand, and me and Grandma held each other's hands. At home, we looked out the window and waited.

Grandma and Mama talked over our heads. "He's somewhere in his cups," said Grandma.

"Don't let the children hear you," Mama cried.

"He's down in the Bottom with those bootleggers and alligators!" Grandma continued.

We know where the Bottom is. One day me and Prince went walking to the Bottom. It was in the swamps with a narrow road leading to a shack with a porch in front. We didn't see any bootleggers or alligators, just men and pretty ladies dancing and having a party. When Mis' Ida saw us, she yelled, "Go away from here or I'll tell your Grandma!" We ran home.

Me and Prince were in bed when Daddy came in, but we weren't asleep. We jumped up to see him. His clothes were muddy. He was drooped and bent-kneed. His eyes were red and his lower lip was swollen. He smelled sour, like stale buttermilk.

"Ruth, put those young'uns to bed," he yelled.

Daddy looked ugly and wild. I was scared.

"Go to your grandma's right away and stay there until I come for you," Mama said.

Grandma put us to bed. Prince slept in Grandpa's bed, and I slept with Grandma.

The next morning, Mama and Grandma were whispering in Grandma's kitchen. We couldn't hear what they were saying.

"Is Daddy going to Eternity?" I asked Prince.

"I told you, dumb Pearl. Daddy is not old and sick," said Prince.

I hit Prince with my bamboo flute and made him cry. He said he was going to tell Reverend Hill not to make any more playthings for me.

"I'm gonna give you young'uns a good whipping if you don't cut out that foolishness," said Grandma.

Mama and Grandma cooked breakfast for

Daddy and took him a bowl of grits with gravy and buttered biscuits. We followed them back to our house. But Daddy wouldn't leave his room. Mama begged, "Eat something, Joe. Get your strength back."

Reverend Hill came to see about Daddy. He put his arm around Mama's shoulder and said, "Joe is a strong man being tested by life. He's no backslider. He's just stumbled a mite." He patted our heads and said, "Be good and help your mama, children."

Even Mr. Moss came to our house. He's the one laid Daddy off.

He told Grandma and Mama that his sawmill business was falling apart—going broke. "The house-building boom has dried up with the Depression. Cement blocks are replacing lumber."

Grandma had always said Mr. Moss was known as a right-thinking white man. She once told us, "He made your daddy foreman over other white and colored workers because he knew your daddy had powerful and steady hands that didn't fumble with those razor-sharp blades." Grandma had also said the Depression was a plague on this land. "It's withering up this town and the people are weary."

After Mr. Moss finished talking 'bout the mill going broke, he gave Daddy's wages to Mama. Daddy didn't leave the room to speak to Mr. Moss.

"Joe is under the weather today," Mama said.

Later, Daddy came out of his room and washed his face and brushed his teeth. He leaned on the kitchen table for a long time before saying anything. He asked Mama for a cool cloth to put on his swollen lip. We crowded around him, but he didn't pay attention to us. He spoke to Mama. "Ruth, I'm leaving this sorry town."

"You have a family and friends, Joe."

We didn't make any noise that day. Mama and Grandma tiptoed around and whispered stuff about Daddy.

When night fell Mama called, "Time for bed, children. Wash your face and hands and your feet and legs."

That night we took a little bird bath in the basin and dumped the dirty water in the tall grass. Then we put on the sleepwear Mama laid out for us.

We slept in old clothes Mama and Daddy used to wear before they got us. They were skinny then.

"Kneel and say your prayers. Ask God to make Daddy feel better and help us all."

We kneeled and prayed for Daddy.

When we got in bed, Mama talked with us like she always did. "We're in a little trouble, but it'll be over soon. You'll see."

"When is Daddy gonna leave this sorry town?"

Mama shook her head. "When the time comes, we'll leave together."

"How did Daddy's face get smashed out of shape?"

Mama's eyes filled with tears and they rolled down her cheeks.

She whispered, "Maybe he got beat up at that moonshine distillery where he used to hang out when you were babies."

"Nobody can beat Daddy! He's big and strong," said Prince.

"Moonshine makes strong people weak and foolish," Mama said.

"Is Daddy weak and foolish, Mama?" I asked.

"No, no, he's worried because he lost his job. Go to sleep now."

Mama sat in her rocking chair between our two cots and stayed there a long time.

MAMA AND DADDY'S QUARREL

Our kingdom fell after Daddy lost his job.

He kept grumbling and mumbling, "This town is no good for a colored man. I'm going up north to find a job!"

Mama said, "Stop worrying, Joe."

"Prince, we're going up north," I said.

"Yeah, we're gonna ride on the train to the North," said Prince.

Daddy complained, "I can't stand this pine-tree swamp of a town. It's strangling me."

He stopped laughing and joking with Mama. He stopped playing boxing and horse riding with us. He wouldn't lift us and toss us over his shoulders.

He sat on the back porch, like he was hiding. His head hung covered in his big hands. Every

now and then he looked up to squirt out a long stream of tobacco juice into the flowerbed Mama had planted. The flowers turned brown and flopped to the ground.

We stood behind an orange tree and peeked at him.

When he saw us watching him, he barked, "Stop staring at me! Your mama should be home by now. Look down the road to see if she's coming."

Mama had to work now at the bakery downtown. We ran out to the road to look and ran back to tell Daddy we didn't see her. The sun was going down, trickling away the summer heat.

Daddy put supper on the table and told us to wash up and bring in a bucket of cool water.

He'd cooked lima beans and rice for supper. It didn't taste good.

"I don't like this supper, Daddy."

"Eat it! Eat it! And be thankful!" said Daddy.

He didn't see me and Prince spitting the stuff from our mouths and pushing it under our plates. When we cleared the table we put the stuff with the chicken scraps.

"Daddy, when are we going up north?" I asked.

"As soon as I get a hold of some money to buy the tickets out of this alligator pit. Now go to your grandma's and pester her!" he hollered.

We stood still and stared at our daddy. He was not like he used to be.

"Your mama should be home taking care of her family!" Daddy shouted.

When Mama came home, she brought boxes of cinnamon buns and cupcakes for our dessert.

Daddy pushed his aside and yelled, "Ruth, you come strolling in here like you don't have a family to look after."

"What more do you want from me?" asked Mama.

"Bring your behind home instead of loitering with those busybodies at the bakery."

Mama threw the box of cinnamon buns at Daddy, but he caught it and looked at Mama for a while. Then he left the table and sat on the porch in the dark.

Mama was shaking and looking outside!

"Time for bed, children," Mama said.

"Soon as we get through washing our feet and legs, Mama."

"Don't forget to brush all that sugar from your teeth," she continued.

I was so glad Mama was home with us. She sat between us in her rocker. "What's on your minds?" she said.

Prince asked, "Where is up north, Mama?"

She got up and walked to the open window.

"Look, see that star, the brightest one shining way out yonder? That's the North Star. We follow it."

"Is Grandma coming with us?" I asked.

"No, no. Your grandma will never move from this town where she holds on to memories of your grandpa."

"Will Daddy get a good job up north?"

"We'll have to wait and see when we get there," Mama said.

"Mama, are you sad?" I asked.

Mama closed her eyes and stopped talking.

"Talk, Mama, talk." I sat on her lap and pressed her face.

"Mama, how come Daddy is so mean?" Prince asked.

Mama's eyes got all teary and she answered, "Your daddy's not mean. He's shaken and rattled. He thinks he's no 'count, 'cause he can't take care of us."

When we were quiet in bed we heard Mama and Daddy quarreling.

"I'll send for you when I'm settled."

"I'm going with you! Mama will help out. She'll lend us the money."

"I am not going to ask your mama for money!" Daddy yelled.

Me and Prince jumped from our beds and listened through the crack in the wall.

"I'm going with you," Mama said again. "I can work. I'll open a café and serve down-home cooking for our people."

They talked low for a while; then I heard Mama say, "Yes, we'll go to the bank."

MR. RANDALL,

THE BANKER

Mama called us early the next morning. "Wake up and put on your Sunday clothes. We're going downtown to the bank."

Grandma had made Prince and me new Sunday outfits. Mine was a pink organdy dress with a sash, and Prince had a blue suit with a sailor collar. Mama said, "Don't you look swell!"

Daddy was wearing his blue serge suit with a white shirt and yellow tie. Mama kept telling him how handsome he looked. Daddy was grumbling, frowning, and sweating a lot. "This monkey suit is too hot. I would rather take a freight train out of here. If I didn't have you and the children, Ruth, I would be long gone from this suffocating town."

"Joe, you have us for better or worse," Mama said.

"Where are my clean overalls?" Daddy asked.

"They are not ironed," said Mama. Her voice was soft and trembly.

Grandma and Mama wore starched white cotton dresses and straw hats. Their shoes were shiny, just like their pocketbooks.

The bank was a long way from our part of town. We walked on the coarse sandy road leading to the cement sidewalks in front of the white people's fine houses, past the post office and Woolworth's five-and-ten store and the drugstore with tables out front where white people ate ham sandwiches and drank cold lemonade.

Grandma had packed a basket of fried-egg-and-biscuit sandwiches and a juicy orange for each of us. Before going to the bank, we needed to use the restroom at the depot where colored people could go. There we freshened ourselves, ate our lunch, and went on to the bank.

"Mr. Randall, this is my daughter, Ruth, and her husband, J. C. Long. These are my grandchildren, Pearl and Prince."

Mr. Randall was the banker. He waved at us and said, "Howdy."

Right away, Grandma told Mr. Randall 'bout how Daddy had lost his job as foreman at the sawmill, and how he was leaving this town and taking us north to live.

"Joe is a hardworking man, and he keeps his word and pays his debts," Grandma said.

Mama and Daddy stood beside each other. They didn't talk. Daddy's mouth was twisted and he kept pulling on his yellow tie like he was a mouse caught in a trap and choking.

Mr. Randall called Daddy. "Come on over, Joe. How much do you need, and what's your plan for paying it back?"

Daddy was silent till Mama gave him a light nudge and said, "Joe, answer."

"I need enough money to get to Philadelphia with my family. I'll pay the bank first chance I get," Daddy mumbled. The sweat was pouring over his shirt collar and he looked toward the door instead of looking at Mr. Randall.

Mr. Randall gave Grandma a paper and said, "Katie, you have to sign for this loan."

Grandma gave the paper right over to Daddy to sign. Then Mama and Grandma signed and passed it back to Mr. Randall.

Mr. Randall gave Daddy some money and said, "This will pay for two tickets to Philadelphia and a few dollars to help you and Ruth get started." Mama put the money in her pocketbook.

"What about us? What about us?"

They were not gonna buy tickets for me and Prince. They were going to leave us here.

"We're not going up north?" I asked.

I started jumping up and down and screaming loud. Prince was crying, too.

Grandma pulled us close to her and whispered, "Where's your manners?"

"They're little children, Mama," our mama said.

Daddy came over and said, "We'll come for you soon. Your grandma will treat you right."

"We need a little time to get situated," Mama said.

"What is 'situated'?" I asked.

"You said Daddy wouldn't leave us!" Prince said.

"Obey your grandma and help her run the store," Daddy said.

We were not going up north. Mama and Daddy were leaving us.

After we left the bank, Mama and Daddy went shopping to buy suitcases and a warm coat for Mama. We went back to the store with Grandma. She tried to make us laugh.

"Before a cat can lick her paws, you and Prince will be riding a train to Philadelphia."

"Tell us where it is, Grandma," said Prince.

"Let's have a cold drink of Orange Crush and some ginger cake before I tell where Philadelphia is."

Prince opened a tall bottle of the soda and filled glasses for each of us. Grandma cut squares of ginger cake and we sat at her kitchen table.

"Your ma and pa will come for you soon. I know that," Grandma said.

Prince opened a second bottle of cold soda. It was grape.

I ate more ginger cake. "Hurry, Grandma, and tell us about Philadelphia and up north!"

Grandma started telling us, "Philadelphia is far away from this little Florida town hanging between an ocean on the east side and a gulf on the west. The wide fields of water are larger than the land we walk on. The Atlantic Ocean and the Gulf of Mexico spread on and on. You can't see the end."

We put our cake and soda aside so we could understand what she was saying. "Can we drown in all that water?" Prince said.

Grandma told us that hurricanes are born in all that water. "We're safe in my Ark when they gush up and pound this town with splashing, rushing wind and rain. Prince, hand me your tablet and I'll draw a picture of what I'm saying."

Grandma's picture of Florida looked like Daddy's sock pinned on our clothesline. Then Grandma drew a picture of railroad tracks and said, "The train rolls on tracks like this: through lots of little towns and junctions, middle-size towns, down into valleys, over bridges crossing rivers, up mountains till it reaches the top. Then it eases down where the ground levels and stretches outward and onward."

"Tell us again, Grandma. What else?" Prince said.

"You go to sleep, wake up, eat, sleep and eat again, till you're tired of eating and sleeping. Then the conductor calls Washington, D.C.; Baltimore, Maryland; Mason-Dixon Line. You're up north now. The next call is Wilmington,

Delaware. And before you can say 'Rain, rain, go away,' the conductor calls Philadelphia, Pennsylvania. And that's that."

We got up and raced around the room and repeated, "Washington, Maryland, Mason-Dixon Line, Baltimore, Philadelphia. And that's that."

"You'll get it right with more practice," said Grandma.

MAMA AND DADDY
LEAVE US

After Daddy got the money for the tickets to leave this sorry town, he stopped quarreling with Mama and he laughed and talked with me and Prince.

"We'll come back for you as soon as we find a roof to cover all our heads. You understand?"

We helped Daddy gather his handsaws, nails, and hammers and stash them away in his tool shed.

Mama and Grandma washed and ironed Daddy's and Mama's good clothes and packed a suitcase for each.

Daddy grinned and said, "Don't pack that hot monkey suit I wore to the bank last week."

Grandma said she would use their old clothes for making quilts.

The singing voices of men rose above the clinking of bells. Daddy pointed to the pushcart peddlers. "They're hawking their wares, plugging their goods for sale—things to wear, and fresh fruits and vegetables," he said.

Philadelphia was bigger than I had ever dreamed a place could be. I didn't know where to look. The people, cars, and buildings were jumbled together in a mountain heap!

And I was excited to have two homes again: the Promised-Land home with Mama and Daddy, and Grandma's General Store, the Ark, where Grandma will be waiting for us to come back to help her when school is out for the summertime.

The day before they left, Mama went to Mis' Lizzie's Beauty Shop and got her hair pressed with Madam Walker's hair dressing. She was pretty in her new suit and her pressed and crimped hair. She hugged me and Prince every time she passed by us and said, "Time flies, time flies. You'll be with us soon."

Daddy killed and cleaned two poults for Grandma to fry for their lunch box. Grandma's customers lingered to take in the good smells coming from the yeast rolls and teacakes baking in our oven. Grandma packed two shoeboxes with food and candy, and Daddy filled a flower sack with oranges.

Customers stood around and looked at Mama and said, "We're gonna miss you, Ruth."

Daddy said he didn't have the mind to say goodbye to all those people. "I need to cut the tall grass and weeds from around this property."

Mama and Daddy took long baths that leaving day. They left our house smelling like tobacco and Mama's April Showers talcum powder that was sprinkled all over her room.

At the depot we waited a long time for the train to come. We didn't talk. Grandma stood behind me with her hands on my shoulders. Mama and Prince stood beside each other holding hands. Daddy kept turning his gaze from his pocket watch to the railroad tracks. Then we saw the train sputtering steam and smoke. It was a roaring giant. Much bigger than the train that ran by Grandma's store.

The wheels clanked and screeched. The bell *dong-donged* along with the *whoo-hoo* sound of the whistle. I was scared of it, but I wanted to go with Mama and Daddy. I wanted to get on that train and see Philadelphia and up north.

Daddy and Mama squeezed us and kissed our faces. Mama said, "Soon, soon, we'll come back for you. Be good children." Then they climbed onto the train and were swallowed by that long iron giant.

Prince cried out, "I can't see nothing but shadows through those gray windows."

Grandma stood between us and pulled us away. "I don't want to hear any whimpering and sniveling. Your mama and daddy are walking back through those coaches to find the one where colored people are permitted to sit and ride. Here, wipe your runny nose, Prince."

She gave him her handkerchief with crochet on it. Prince blew his nose on Grandma's fancy handkerchief.

"Where are they, Grandma?" I asked.

"They are walking to that last coach at the end of the train. See? Look."

The train began to sputter and spray a lot of steam as it moved forward. Soon the last coach rolled by us and we saw shadows of Mama and Daddy waving and pressing their heads against the cloudy windows.

"We don't want to stay here, Grandma," said Prince.

"We want to go with Mama and Daddy," I said.

"When are they coming back to get us?" asked Prince.

Grandma stood between us, holding our hands, but all she said was "I'm gonna make you some ice cream in the churn when we get to the store. We'll stop at Mr. Mac's fruit stand and buy some soft ripe bananas for flavor."

Instead of going to the store with Grandma

and Prince, I stopped at our house. When I opened the door, I smelled Mama's April Showers talcum powder and Daddy's chewing tobacco. Mama's old pink kimono lay in a pile of soiled clothes on the floor. Mama had bought brand-new clothes to wear up north. I was tired, so I covered myself with Mama's kimono and fell asleep on the pile of clothes.

When I woke up, I listened and looked around for Mama and Daddy. They were gone, really gone.

I went over to Grandma's. Prince was waving the ice cream dasher around. "Pearl, Pearl, I've got the dasher! Grandma left a lot of ice cream on it."

"I don't want any ice cream, Prince," I said.

"We'll save some for you, Pearl," said Grandma.

She packed the churn with chopped ice and salt. "This will keep it nice and firm."

Grandma bathed my face with a soft cool cloth and said, "Get the comb and brush so I can tidy up your hair while I'm sitting here resting my backside."

I sat on a little stool beneath Grandma's lap.

She brushed my hair but she didn't yank or pull it. I didn't feel like crying anymore, so I ate the dish of smooth banana ice cream Grandma gave me. It tasted just like the ice cream Mama made on Sundays after church.

LIVING WITH GRANDMA

Days, weeks, and months passed but Mama and Daddy didn't come for us. Mama wrote a letter but didn't say nothing 'bout coming to take us up north!

Grandma read it out loud:

"Dear Mama, Pearl, and Prince,

We miss you! Your hugs and noisy mouths and Mama's busy, bossy little self. (smile)

People from all over the world are squeezed together in this City of Brotherly Love. That is Philadelphia's nickname. Joe goes out every day doing piddling jobs, but his anger and hot temper have changed for the better. He's hopeful and believes a real job is right around the corner.

I'm the pastry cook at this boardinghouse where we live with Miss Brown, the landlady. We've got a little commissary started where the lodgers can buy extra sweets—cupcakes, cinnamon buns, apple dumplings, and sweet potato pie and peach cobbler. I use your recipes, Mama.

Hug Prince and Pearl for me, and don't worry about me and Joe. We are going to make our lives better!

Much Love,
Ruth and Joe"

I took the letter and looked at it over and over, but I couldn't figure out all Mama was saying. I just wanted to go to Philadelphia.

Grandma let Prince and me help tend the store and told us how much money to charge for everything. We helped her make little signs showing the prices of all the canned goods on the shelf. Del Monte peaches, 15 cents; pork'n'-beans, 10 cents; potted meat, 5 cents; snuff, 5 cents; and Prince Albert tobacco, 10 cents. That's the kind Daddy chewed! It smelled so good.

One day me and Prince bit off a wad and started chewing, but the stuff tasted bitter and made us cough and swallow the juice. That's when we passed out and scared the life out of Grandma. She put her fingers down our throats and made us throw up and splashed water all over us. When we came to, she was shaking us and wiping our mouths. Then she told us to sit on the bench and keep still and quiet. She took a Stanback headache powder. We got tired of sitting on that bench with nothing to do. "Can we get up now, Grandma?" I asked.

She made us sit a long time and said, "If you ever chew another wad, I'll give you a whipping you'll never forget."

Grandma was always muttering riddles. She'd say things like " 'An idle mind is the devil's workshop.' Stop your idling, we've got work to do, children. Pearl, get the ledger from under the counter."

One day Grandma read the pile of "please charge it" notes and showed me where to write the words: Kerosene, 25 cents, Bradshaw. Mr. Bradshaw owed for a lot of charges.

"I sure hope he pays up soon," said Grandma.

Prince packed paper bags with sugar, rice, and dried beans. Then he weighed each bag on the scale with a sliding bar for measuring the pounds. We filled the wagon that Daddy had built for Prince, and off we went to make deliveries. "Come on, Pearl, you push and I'll pull."

"Hurry, children, take the soup up to Mis' King first and put the groceries on her kitchen table. Tell her I hope she's feeling better."

With our loaded wagon, we called out, "All aboard for Philadelphia!"

Before we went to sleep, Grandma told us stories 'bout Mama when she was a little girl and stories 'bout long ago when animals could talk and outsmart each other just like people. But most of all she talked 'bout Grandpa.

"Your grandpa was a forward-looking man. First he built us a house, and then he added on the store. After that he built the house next door where y'all lived. He wanted to guarantee that your mama would always have a roof over her head."

"Where is Grandpa now?" I asked again.

Grandma cleared her throat before talking some more. "He's with the angels in Eternity."

"Your grandpa couldn't tolerate lying and trifling people," she continued.

"I want a drink of water, Grandma," I said.

"I need to use the pot bad, Grandma," said Prince.

"Get going and hurry back so I can finish telling you 'bout your grandpa."

Prince was gone a long time, 'cause he was tired of hearing 'bout Grandpa.

"Did you wash your hands?" she asked Prince.

Prince said he did, but I knew he didn't.

"Grandma, tell us again, where's up north?" Prince asked.

Grandma went to the window and raised the shade. "Let's look for the North Star," she said.

The sky was filled with tiny flashing stars that hid the North Star.

"Grandma, are you looking for the North Star?" I asked.

"Oh, it's up there dangling among that host guiding our paths."

"Tell us again how to go north," I said.

Grandma settled back down in her chair. "Well, the train has to cross over a line that runs between a land called Maryland and a different land called Pennsylvania. The line is called the Mason-Dixon Line. When colored people cross that line into Pennsylvania, all children can walk on sidewalks to schools and get books from the public library—colored children the same as white children."

We heard a rustling in the backyard. Grandma's chickens were flapping about.

"It's that possum after my chickens," said Grandma.

She took a lamp into the kitchen, picked up a piece of firewood, and threw it at the possum.

When she returned to her chair, she asked, "What was I saying?"

"I'm thirsty, Grandma."

"You tired of hearing me talk. Say your prayers and go to sleep."

Grandma pulled the patchwork quilt over me and patted my backside. She gave Prince's foot a little tug and said, "Good night."

I was not sleepy. So many puzzles were

swarming around in my head. I sat up in the bed so I could keep thinking 'bout up north where Mama and Daddy were.

Grandma left the bedroom door open and went into her front room. She sat in her Bible-reading chair next to a small table holding a lamp. She turned up the lamp wick for more light and began reading her Bible out loud. " 'I will lift up mine eyes unto the hills, from whence cometh my help. My help cometh from the Lord.' "

Through the open window sounds of crickets, cats, and dogs joined into a night choir singing with the soft breeze.

Grandma fell asleep in her chair. I wanted her to come to bed and give me a hug. She was so little and strong.

"Prince, I love Grandma! Do you?"

"Yeah, I do. Why you ask that? You sound dumb, Pearl!"

"Do you still love our mama and daddy, too?"

"Yeah, yeah, I do. But they're too far away."

"I want to see them, Prince. Do you think they remember us?"

"Yeah, Pearl. They remember us. And I love Grandma, too."

"Good night, Prince."

"G'night, Pearl."

Early next morning a heavy banging on our front door awakened us. Grandma sat upright in her bed and mumbled, "Who in the name of tarnation is that banging this early?" She wrapped the bedspread around her flannel nightgown and went to the door. "Who is it, who is it?"

Then we heard Reverend Hill's voice. "Mis' Katie, you and the children get dressed as quick as you can!" We were standing behind Grandma. Reverend Hill whispered, "The Klansmen are riding this way. Bo Bringy is running around spreading the news."

Soon another voice called, "Mis' Katie, the Klansmen are coming!" The voice was Mr. Bo Bringy's. We dressed in a hurry, and Grandma told us to go wash our faces and hands.

When we returned to the bedroom Grandma was pulling out a shiny-handled pistol from her sewing basket under her bed. She was breaking it open and looking at parts of it. When she saw me and Prince standing there she shoved the pistol back into the basket and told us to sit on Grandpa's bed. "Keep your mouths shut."

"Grandma," Prince asked, "is that a real gun?"

We were used to seeing the men with rifles going hunting for rabbits, and we had play guns carved from tree branches. But we had never seen Grandma with a gun.

"Grandma, why you hiding it?"

"Don't you ever touch that thing or speak a word about it to anyone, you hear me?"

"Show it to us again, Grandma," begged Prince.

"It's a dangerous and devilish thing that can do serious harm to people. Forget you saw it." Grandma sounded angry, so me and Prince didn't ask to see it again.

After we collected ourselves, all washed and dressed, we went outside to see what was happening.

Crowds were standing around in front of the store and people were arriving slowly from every which way. Reverend Hill, Mr. Bo Bringy, and his wife, Mis' Bessie, were in the crowd. Mis' Bessie was Grandma's friend. Grandma says she's a hardworking washerwoman with a good heart, and she saves her money.

The people didn't talk or smile or walk around but stood as if they were planted like pine trees.

"Look, Prince, here comes the parade."

Grandma gave me a jerk and said, "Hush."

There were about twelve riders all covered in white robes with white hoods over their heads. Their heads looked like ghost faces with dark pits for eyes and mouths.

I whispered, "Is this Halloween, Grandma?"

"Quiet, child!"

The riders stopped their horses in front of the store and formed a large circle in the road.

One rider moved into the center; another followed, and the first moved back to the rim of the circle. The riders kept changing places until each rider had been to the center and back again. After that they trotted their horses in and out of winding curves and circles. The riders stood still for a while with their ghost faces

turned toward where we stood with Grandma. We were the only children in the crowd. Maybe the other children didn't want to see the parade. One of the riders spoke to Prince. "Boy, do you know how to cut the buck?"

"What's that, Grandma?" Prince asked.

Reverend Hill answered, "The child doesn't know how to dance, sir."

The next thing the riders did was to make the horses stand on their hind legs, neigh, and bare their big teeth. The people in the crowd were still as gravestones.

"Are they circus riders, Grandma?" Prince asked. Grandma held us close.

A rider asked, "How y'all like that?"

Grandma mumbled, "Boy-men practicing their meanness."

Another rider spoke. "We hope y'all enjoyed our little show. These are our new steeds and we're training them. Y'all are good Nigras. You don't have nothing to worry about from us. Ain't that right, Hill?"

Reverend Hill answered, "Amen."

Grandma's hold on me and Prince tightened.

"That's Colonel Snipes, the Grand Wizard,

talking," Reverend Hill whispered to Grandma.

The twelve hooded men rode off, with their horses kicking up clouds of dust behind them.

Mis' Bessie groaned. "Lord, I'm the one got to wash all those filthy robes again. I'd quit working for Colonel Snipes if Mis' Snipes hadn't been so kind to me and my children before she got sick!"

The people walked away slowly in different directions just like they were going to a funeral.

Reverend Hill called the parade the devil's work. He told Prince 'bout cutting the buck, or buck dancing. "It's cutting capers, making a fool of yourself. You must never stoop to that, my child."

Grandma took us back to her room where the pistol was hidden. She sat in her rocker and sang softly, " 'His eyes are on the sparrow, and I know He watches me.' "

"Grandma, are we gonna shoot someone with that thing?" asked Prince.

"No, child. No! It was your grandpa's. He got a hold of it after some bad men burned a cross in front of this house. They were trying to scare him from buying this little property he was adding up. If a colored man owned property, he could vote."

"What's voting, Grandma?" asked Prince.

Grandma was slow answering but finally said, "It's choosing something or someone you like, the way you always choose fried chicken over boiled chicken and dumplings." Then she continued, "Your grandpa wasn't going to be scared off. The very next day he put on his Sunday best, including his black fedora hat, and went to see Judge Mel Griffin at the city courthouse. He and your grandpa were children together and played in the Griffins' house and yard. Your great-grandma Katherine was the cook for the Griffins. They were well-to-do white people. Judge Griffin and your grandpa remained friends.

"When your grandpa told Judge Griffin about the cross burning, the judge got raging mad. He gave your grandpa the pistol and told him to shoot it up in the air and scare the living daylights out of the riffraff if they should ever come back. Your grandpa had no cause to ever use it, and by and by we felt safe again. We never had any more trouble. The pistol has been lying at the bottom of my basket ever since. Never tell anyone what I've just told you or what you have seen. You hear me? You hear me?"

"Can we tell Mama and Daddy when they come for us?" asked Prince.

Grandma squinted and said, "We'll tell them together."

Prince went out to the porch and looked at the clawed-up road left by the horses. Later we helped Reverend Hill rake the road smooth again.

SUMMER WAS LONG

Reverend Hill stopped by Grandma's store nearly every day.

"Just thought I'd drop by to see how you and the children are getting along, Mis' Katie."

"Thank you, Reverend."

When he went outside to wash his hands at the pump, Grandma whispered, "He can sniff my home cooking miles away. His heart is right, but he's so long-winded."

He showed me and Prince how to make kites with the spines of palmetto leaves by tying the spines into a kite frame, then covering it with brown wrapping paper. He also made Tom Walkers; they were broom-handle stilts. You nailed an empty tin can to each handle, and then you stood on the cans between the two handles and lifted yourself forward.

Sometimes he carved flutes from bamboo shoots and whistled bird songs that sounded like real mourning doves.

Grandma would make a skillet of egg bread for our lunch, and Reverend Hill would bow his head and say a long blessing.

Grandma's store was also a resting stop for Mis' Lucille, Mis' Bessie, Mis' Ernestine, and Mis' Ada. They stopped by on their way home from their cooking and housecleaning jobs across town where the rich white people lived.

"It feels so good to sit here and rest for a spell," said Mis' Ada.

"That's the living truth, honey," said Mis' Bessie.

"That long walk 'cross town is wearing me down," said Mis' Lucille.

"My hands ache from all that washing, ironing, scrubbing, and lifting young'uns—and then doing the same things when I get home," said Mis' Bessie.

"Wrap a bottle of that Sloan's Liniment, Pearl. I'll rub my knees before I go to bed," said Mis' Lucille.

The women fanned themselves with their handmade palmetto fans.

Grandma called us aside and said, "I want you to be seen and not heard. Understand? Keep your mouths closed tight like this (she squeezed her lips together) when grown people are talking."

"Grandma, your face looks silly when you squish it that way," I said.

"Don't you talk back when I'm telling you how to behave yourself!" Grandma said.

The resting women talked secrets that we didn't know. They talked a lot about Grandma's other customers. They called Mis' Ida "a brazen hussy and a disgrace." They said, "She dances the shimmy-shimmy every Saturday night at the Bottom and then sings in the choir on Sunday mornings."

"Pearl, hand me a bottle of that cold soda water from your grandma's icebox, if you don't mind," said Mis' Ada.

"Get us all a bottle while you're at it, Pearl," said Mis' Ernestine. I looked at Grandma to see if I should pass out her soda water to the resting women. She nodded.

"Katie, don't worry—you'll get paid on Saturday payday," promised Mis' Bessie. She called me and Prince. "Come here, children, and let me get a close look at you. Both of you are the spitting image of your mama. Pearl has her mama's good-looking features and thick head of hair. And, Prince, you're gonna be big and tall like your daddy."

"Katie, when are Ruth and Joe coming to get their young'uns?" asked Mis' Lucile.

"Has Joe found a job up north yet? I don't see how they could leave their young children for you to raise 'em at your age," said Mis' Ada.

Mis' Lucille added, "My ol' man can't find a job either, but we're staying right here, where we have toiled and sweated all our lives. Get the comb and brush, Pearl, and I'll braid your hair while I'm sitting here resting my tired bones."

Grandma stood up, took my hand, and said, "I'm gonna do Pearl's hair soon as I get time." Then she frowned and threw up her hands. "My young'uns are just fine and dandy."

Grandma didn't talk and laugh with the

women anymore that day. After they left, she put her hands on her hips, swayed back, and snapped, "Doggone it, these folk must think my store is Noah's Ark and I'm Mis' Noah."

"Are those bad words, Grandma?" asked Prince.

"No, child, go feed the chickens. Pearl, fetch me a Stanback headache powder and a glass of ice water. That worry headache is here again."

I wrapped some ice in a cloth and put it on her forehead.

After her worry headache went away, Grandma combed and plaited my hair. "I can't have you going around here looking like an orphan."

Grandma cooked at the back of the store. She asked, "Who'd like apple fritters for supper?"

"Me, me!" said Prince.

"I would, I would, Grandma."

She stirred up a batter with eggs, milk, flour, and dried apples and dropped spoonfuls in sizzling grease. We had cold lemonade with the fritters.

"Grandma, these fritters melt in my mouth. How you make 'em so light and puffed up?"

"Not much in them but hot air, like some people."

While we were eating, Grandma told us for the hundredth time about Grandpa.

"Your grandpa was a forward-looking man. He scrimped and saved up enough money from his little sawmill wages to get this store started, and he built the house next door for your mama. Your daddy paid good rent when he worked at the sawmill."

"Grandma, when are we going to Philadelphia?" asked Prince.

"Not until your ma and pa can take care of you as well as I can," she snapped.

"I'm thirsty for water, Grandma," I said.

"Get your water and come back to the table," she said. Grandma was going to keep talking about Grandpa. "Your grandpa would've loved you young'uns mightily."

"If Grandpa was here, Daddy could still work at the sawmill, I bet," said Prince.

"Grandma, why don't they come for us?" I asked.

"Oh, you children worry me! Life ain't easy in big towns like Philadelphia. Your ma and pa are trying to learn new ways to live as best they can. They love you the same as I do! So let that soak into your hard heads."

Grandma winked and patted our heads.

One day that summer, Prince said, "Let's run away to Philadelphia to see our mama and daddy."

So we set out walking along the railroad tracks that passed by Grandma's store.

We couldn't see the North Star in the bright daylight.

We walked on and on under the scorching sun until we came to a trestle. It stretched over a muddy stream of water splashing over large jagged rocks and leaping catfish and eels. We got scared of falling, but we were about to cross over when we heard the train whistle blow.

The train was puffing out big caterpillars of smoke and chugging behind us. It slowed, and the trainman leaned out his engine window and waved for us to get off the tracks. We stood for a second, too scared to move. The train kept com-

ing and the engine man kept waving and hollering at us. We grabbed each other and leaped down into a patch of thorny blackberry bushes.

After the train roared by, we scrambled out of the bushes and ran back to Grandma's as fast as we could.

"We're gonna get a good whipping, Prince," I said.

"Don't tell Grandma, Pearl," said Prince.

When we got home, we were out of breath and our legs were scratched and bleeding.

Grandma was sitting on the front porch in her big rocking chair, taking turns nodding, snoring, and waking up to patch and mend our freshly washed and ironed everyday clothes. "What you young'uns up to? You go mind the store till I get done patching your clothes," she said.

We were safe back in the Ark and out of trouble. If we had kept going across that trestle, maybe we would have fallen into Eternity. That's where our grandpa was. Grandma said people get healing there. Grandpa had an accident at the sawmill and went to Eternity to get his hurt leg healed. But we just wanted to go to Philadelphia and see our mama and daddy.

IT'S HURRICANE TIME

A mild breeze cooled the air around us. Grandma stood on her porch and gazed up at the churning clouds. "It's that time. I can feel it in my bones, children."

In the tall grasses near Grandma's store, the crickets, grasshoppers, and bobwhites quit chirping and calling. "Come, children, help Grandma put props on the side of the chicken house." The chickens were cackling and running around like they were dizzy. "They know it's hurricane time," said Grandma.

Reverend Hill and some deacons from our church nailed boards across the windows of Grandma's store and house. The men hoisted the heavy burlap sacks of chicken feed onto wooden crates. We pulled out pots, pans, and buckets to catch water in case Grandma's tin

roof leaked. "I sure hope it holds together," she said.

The hurricane came rumbling and rolling through the town, twisting trees and breaking electric lines. Daylight turned dark and the water swelled in the lakes and spilled over the land. The water rolled into our store up to our knees. Reverend Hill prayed, "Thy will be done, Lord!"

We huddled near the door. Grandma tied her big apron around us. "Hold on to me!" We grabbed her waistband. "Is God talking, Grandma?"

"Are we gonna be blown away?" asked Prince.

The strong wind ripped open the back of the tin roof. The pieces clanged and flung about, letting in the drenching rain. I yelled, "Grandma, the water is rising over me."

Prince yelled, "I can't walk!"

Grandma dragged us closer to the open door. We looked out and saw houses shaken into woodpiles. People were running and stumbling in the rushing water packed with fallen trees.

Reverend Hill grabbed Prince, and Grandma

squeezed me tighter. "Hold on, Mis' Katie! Hold on, children! I'm here beside you."

We could hear tin tubs, buckets, chimney bricks, and house shingles zooming through the air like daggers and bullets. Clamped in Grandma's arms and apron, I whispered to Prince, "Is the hurricane reaching where Mama and Daddy live up north?"

Prince whispered back, "Hurricanes can't go that far."

Soon, people were pushing and shoving themselves through the cracked door to find shelter in the store.

"Mis' Katie's store is our Ark, our shelter in this mighty storm!" said Reverend Hill.

We waited a long time for the rain and the wind to let up. We had to go without clean drinking water because we couldn't get to the pump. Grandma gave the people most of the rations in her store. The stores downtown could not be reached through the high waters.

After the wild winds became still, the sun burst out like a billowing reddish dragon. The sandy soil swallowed the water, leaving dead fish, stinking chickens, and the bodies of dogs and cats. Side by side with Grandma we raked and cleaned the chopped-up yard and road.

"Watch out for broken glass and rusty nails!" Grandma warned.

Reverend Hill and his deacons came along with shovels. "We're gonna dig a pit on that empty lot so we can bury the sight of all that destruction. Once more we've come through trials and tribulations."

Grandma whispered, "I sure hope the Reverend won't talk too long."

The deacons worked and talked right along with Reverend Hill.

"Oh, we've been through a mighty perilous storm, but we're still here with our faith and spirits renewed!"

Grandma said, "I thank you, Reverend, and all you deacons for helping us get through. Next thing, winter will be here before you can say snapdragon." They laughed and kept cleaning up the dead stuff.

Deacon James climbed the ladder and nailed down the roof that had been cut loose by the wind.

The men looked around the store, the

house, and the yard. The chicken coop was still propped up. Some chickens were still alive, though soaked and dripping, their feet locked onto their perches. Others had fallen and had drowned in the muddy water. Their legs were sticking up and their eyes were wide open.

Reverend Hill shook his head as he shoveled up the stiff chickens and buried them in the pit on the empty lot. He looked down the road at the piles of split trees and shattered houses and said, "In this life we have to take the bitter with the sweet: 'To every thing there is a season, and a time to every purpose under heaven.' "

The clouds turned from dark gray pigs into pale blue floating horses.

Inside the store, we had lots of work to do. We opened the doors and windows to let in the fresh air and sunshine.

Grandma said, "Thank you, Lord. My little Ark is still anchored!"

She talked riddles!

THE SCHOOL

ON THE OTHER SIDE
OF TOWN

Grandma's customers kept asking, "Katie, why don't you send Pearl and Prince to school?"

Grandma frowned and said, "When they go up north to live with their mama and daddy, they'll go to school. Meanwhile, they're learning to read, write, do figures, and behave themselves right here, where I can keep my eyes on them."

Mis' Bessie talked on. "Katie, I know the children are company for you since Joe and Ruth went up north to live. Prince and Pearl help you in the store, but if they were mine I would send them to school."

Grandma started squinting and blinking her eyes and rubbing her forehead. "Bessie, you do what's best for your young'uns, and I'll do the same for mine."

Grandma let us practice our lessons with the Webster's Blue-Back Speller and the slate that belonged to our mama when she was a child. We could even read the old McGuffey Readers.

But Mis' Bessie shook her head and said, "Schooling's the only chance they've got out of these laundry tubs and orange trees." Mis' Bessie's hands had big knots on the backs of her fingers from scrubbing on tin washboards.

"I know that's backbreaking work for penny-pinching wages," Grandma replied. She looked worried, but she turned to us and said, "You young'uns are going to school up north, you understand?"

"When, Grandma? When are we going?" I asked.

"How come we can't go to school right now, Grandma?" said Prince.

And then one day Grandma let us go to school with C.H. and Sam, who lived down the road. The school for colored children was way over on the other side of town. We had to walk through a wide cow field thick with prickly palmetto bushes, spiky cockleburs, and wet, smelly cow pies. Along the way other children joined the walk to school—big children and little children, like me and Prince.

I held my new dress close to my legs to keep the prickers from tearing it. Grandma had just finished making it the night before. It was gingham, checked with red, blue, and yellow.

When Sam slid on some wet grass, his shoes got messed up with cow dung. The other children laughed at him and held their noses. Sam said a bad word and wiped his shoe on the grass.

After crossing the field, we walked beside it a long time on the grassy side of the highway. It was crowded with trucks stacked high with crates of oranges. Other big trucks carried cows in pens. Suddenly a cow truck ran off the road. The pens broke, letting the cows run wild. The children scattered every which way. C.H. and Sam grabbed me and Prince and shouted, "Run for the fence!"

We squeezed under the barbwire fence around the cow field. The barbwire ripped a sleeve of my new dress, got tangled in my hair, and scratched my neck. Prince got his pants and underwear snagged wide open to his bare backside.

We lost our writing tablets and big red pencils with shiny black words that said, "What I am to be, I'm now becoming."

We couldn't go on to school with our clothes ruined, so we turned toward home by ourselves.

Prince led the way, yelling, "Run, Pearl!"

Cow stuff was everywhere, but this time we didn't tiptoe and watch our steps across the field. We ran and leaped over thick bushes and fallen tree branches. I lost my balance and skidded into a pile of nasty, smelly stuff. I thought we'd never get out of the wide, grassy tunnels of tall weeds.

I followed Prince until we saw the store. Then we called out, "Grandma! Grandma! Something happened."

Grandma rushed out, looking scared and sick. "What in the name of the devil . . . ?" Her voice was soft and weak.

We told her 'bout the truck turning over, letting the cows loose, and how we had to run for our lives, and got our clothes torn up and lost our tablets and pencils, and how Sam and C.H. went on to school.

Prince said, "I led the way out of the cow field back home. And we ran fast, Grandma."

Tears rolled down her cheeks. She pulled us into her arms and said, "Your schooldays in this town are finished." She helped us haul water for our baths and gave us clean clothes. "What a shame! What a shame!" Then she took her Stanback headache powder and calmed down.

After our baths she put Vaseline on our scratches and combed and brushed my hair. "Go soak those filthy clothes, and I'll wash and mend them tomorrow."

When we went out to the wash shed, I asked Prince, "Do you still want to go to school?"

He waited for a while and said, "I do, yes, and I don't, no."

I wanted to see what real school was like, but Grandma's store became our school and she was our teacher.

That afternoon, Sam and C.H. stopped by the store to offer to take us to school again. "Mis' Katie, we won't walk through that cow field and on the highway to get to school no more," said Sam. "We'll go along the railroad tracks. The train don't come till afternoon, when we're in school. We won't get run over."

Grandma sank into her quiet way and told Sam and C.H. to help themselves to some full-moon cookies and soda water. With their treats they sat on the bench and waited for Grandma's answer.

I wanted to know whether Grandma was going to send us to school that way.

She said, "Sam, C.H., you know how to skirt dangers, but my young'uns haven't learned how to take on those dangerous trips like walking on the railroad tracks."

Grandma's body slumped, and she looked tired and little.

I said, "I don't want to go to school, Grandma."

Prince said, "I don't want to go to school either, Grandma."

Sam and C.H. left, and we ate baloney sandwiches and oranges at the back of the store. Grandma was still resting her mind. She didn't eat her sandwich. She rubbed her hands a lot and shook her head. She looked sad.

I asked, "Grandma, how come we can't go

to that brick school on the paved street downtown?"

She didn't answer.

"How come? How come we can't go to that school where the white children go?" I continued.

" 'Cause you ain't white! That's why," Grandma snapped.

Prince was still and quiet, but he was looking at Grandma and listening. He said, "Grandma, you've got a lot of white on you. Can't you take us?"

Grandma laughed and said, "I'm yaller . . . I'm a yaller colored woman. Your daddy is a yaller colored man. Not yellow like butter, but yaller like punkins." Grandma laughed some more and almost choked. "Get me a glass of water, Prince." Her face turned red and her eyes filled with tears. "When I was a child, my playmates called me 'yaller punkin, yaller punkin.' They were poking fun at me because I stood out and got a lot of attention. My own mama and daddy called me a 'pretty lil' yaller gal.' When I grew bigger, I didn't like being noticed that way, but Mama and Daddy said we should not fret

over being different. It's nature's way of showing her wonders and miracles. Every child is a
wonder and a miracle."

Mama, Prince, and me are brown like
chocolate pudding. "Was Grandpa a yaller colored man?" I asked.

Grandma smiled again and said, "Oh, no. He
was the color of blackberries, and blackberry
sweet. My, oh my." Grandma's wrinkles flat-
tened, making her face look smooth. It beamed,
and she threw her head back and laughed out
loud. She said, "Colored people are black,
brown, tan, yaller, and light skinned. Some colored people even look white. You can't tell the
difference . . ."

Prince asked, "How come if some colored
people look white, they're colored?"

Grandma cleared her throat and said, "Long
time ago, some wrongheaded white men made
rules for deciding who is white, black, red, yellow, and colored—and what race you belong to,
and your chances to become what you want to
be."

Prince asked, "How you get to be a rule
maker, Grandma?"

Grandma paused for a long time and said,

"Rule making is hard. But you remember that the Bible teaches us to treat others the way we want to be treated. Everyone wants to be respected."

Prince hopped up and strutted and said, "I'm gonna be a fair brown rule maker. I'm gonna make a rule to let colored children go to schools with sidewalks." Then he asked again, "Grandma, how you get to be a rule maker?"

"You've got to be extra smart in your books, don't be a liar, and stay out of trouble. That is how you begin," said Grandma.

But Prince didn't stay out of trouble. He did a wrong thing that made Grandma scream and faint. A few days after we saw that dangerous thing hidden under Grandma's bed, he took it out of the sewing basket and went behind the chicken coop, and I heard him saying, "Bang! Bang!"

I was at the pump getting a bucket of water. I didn't see the dangerous thing until I went behind the chicken coop where he was pointing it up in the air and trying to pull down the shooting trigger. I forgot about the water when I saw Prince playing with that pistol.

"You're not supposed to touch that thing," I said. "Grandma told us to forget we ever saw it!"

From the house Grandma called, "Hurry with the water, Pearl."

Prince dropped his arm and ran in to Grandma's bedroom. When I caught up, he was on his knees sneaking the pistol back in its hiding place. But just then, Grandma walked in and saw the dangerous thing in Prince's hand. That is when she fainted and fell on Grandpa's bed. Her eyes were rolled back and her mouth was open and dripping slobber.

I ran back to the pump, brought in the bucket, and patted some water on Grandma's face. She woke up and said, "Go get Reverend Hill."

Prince didn't move. His eyes were big as toad frogs and the tears were pouring down his face. I ran as fast as a jackrabbit to the parsonage. Reverend Hill was reading his Bible and drinking coffee. I told him what Prince had done and that Grandma wanted him to come at once.

When Reverend Hill got to our house, Grandma was sitting down, moaning and fanning herself. Reverend Hill told her to calm down. Prince was standing behind Grandma's chair. His face was smudged with dirty tears.

Grandma pulled out the sewing basket and told Reverend Hill to take the pistol away. "I never want to see it again. It's a rattlesnake in my house."

Reverend Hill put the pistol in his pocket and asked where it came from.

Grandma told us to go take care of the store, but it was too early for customers. I stood outside Grandma's room and listened to what she told Reverend Hill 'bout the time Judge Griffin gave Grandpa the pistol so he could scare off the riffraff who burned a cross in our yard to keep Grandpa from buying land.

I heard Reverend Hill say, "Mis' Katie, you can't rightfully blame that child for all that evil."

Grandma asked Reverend Hill to get her headache powder and a glass of water from her washstand.

I kept listening as I moved to the front porch, where Prince sat on the steps whimpering with his head hanging down.

"Grandma says you are hard-headed, Prince!"

Grandma was raving and ranting like a wild woman.

"Prince, Grandma said she's gonna whip you within an inch of your life."

"I'm gonna run away! To Philadelphia!" Prince said.

"Prince, you know Grandma is just saying that. She always forgets to give us a whipping."

Reverend Hill said we were nosy young'uns. "We have to watch over them, Katie, and keep harm and evil out of their reach," he said.

When Reverend Hill left, Grandma came on the porch and sat beside me in our swing. Prince was still sitting on the steps with his head hanging.

"Come here, Prince, and give me a hug."

Prince looked shamefaced, but he stumbled up the steps and put his arms around Grandma's neck before sitting with us in the swing. We were quiet till Grandma said, "We've learned a hard lesson, children."

"Yes, ma'am, Grandma," said Prince.

SHOES FOR WINTER

"Put on your Sunday pants, Prince! Pearl, you wear your blue muslin with the white tucking," Grandma called to us. "We're going downtown to buy shoes for you."

We'd gone barefoot all summer long and had outgrown last year's shoes.

"Jack Frost will be here soon," said Grandma. "He's on his way."

The weather was still warm, though, as we walked downtown on the dirt roads and cement sidewalks. When we met Mis' Hattie, one of Grandma's customers, I told her we were going to buy new shoes.

"Y'all are dressed so fine," she said.

Before going inside Mr. Pearson's shoe store, Grandma patted down my hair and straightened Prince's pants.

At the store, boxes of shoes were stacked to the ceiling. Mr. Pearson had to climb a ladder to get two pairs of brown oxfords for us.

"These will fit 'em fine, Katie." He gave us a rag and said, "Wipe the dust off those feet."

Grandma looked in her pocketbook and said she forgot to bring our socks.

Prince squeezed into the oxfords and said, "Grandma, these shoes hurt!"

"They'll stretch, boy, as you wear them," promised Mr. Pearson.

"He needs a bigger size, Mr. Pearson. He's growing mighty fast."

Mr. Pearson brought down a bigger pair of shoes for Prince.

"How do those feel?" Grandma asked.

"They don't hurt," said Prince.

Mr. Pearson gave me a pair of ugly brown oxfords just like the ones Prince had on.

"These shoes are ugly. I want patent leather shoes with ankle straps, Grandma," I said.

"Hush your mouth, child," said Grandma. Then she turned to the owner of the store. "Mr. Pearson, I can't pay you for the shoes to-day, but as soon as I receive the money from my daughter and her husband up north, I'll pay you."

"That's fine with me, Katie. Your word is your bond," Mr. Pearson said.

We left the store wearing our new shoes without any socks. They rubbed blisters on my heels. When I got home, I popped the blisters and painted my sore heels with Mercurochrome.

Jack Frost didn't stay long like summer did. Still, the early mornings were freezing. We hated to leave our warm beds, but Grandma made us get up.

"Hurry and put your clothes on, and bring in some fresh water." We got dressed under the covers.

Icicles dangled from the pump. We knocked them into the bucket and pumped and pumped till the water flowed.

The grass was frozen as hard as spikes of glass. Our ugly brown oxfords were handy. When the sun came out, we helped Grandma cover her sapling orange trees with burlap. Grandma said the Florida freeze was hard on her young orange trees. Then we fetched the chicks inside the chicken coop. Prince ran around scooping them up while I shooed away the mama hen.

"Don't let that hen peck me, Pearl."

One day when we were working in the store putting rations on the shelves, the truant man stopped by to see Grandma. "Grandma, Mr. Truant Man wants to speak to you."

He looked at me and Prince and asked, "How old are you?"

I answered, "I'm going on six and Prince is seven."

"How come you ain't in school?" he asked.

"Grandma won't 'low us to go to school again," said Prince.

Grandma was in back of the store ripping apart Grandpa's old suit jackets to make warm coats for me and Prince.

"Come on back, Mr. Tyson," said Grandma.

Mr. Tyson sat at our eating table.

"Make yourself comfortable, Mr. Tyson."

"Katie, do you have any of your famous ginger cake around?"

Grandma gave him a piece of the leftover cake. It was still soft and moist. He helped himself to a bottle of soda water. He didn't hurry at all.

We listened from behind the shelves to find out if he was gonna make us go to school or take Grandma to jail. Mr. Tyson reared back in Grandma's resting chair and sipped his soda.

Grandma squeezed her forehead and said, "Careful, Mr. Tyson. You are one big heavy-set white man, you know that, don't you? Wouldn't take much rearing to break the legs off that little chair."

Mr. Tyson laughed and said, "Excuse me, Katie. I didn't mean to break up your chair." He sat up straight and ate his cake and sipped his soda. "Katie, how come you ain't sending your young'uns to school? You're supposed to stand for something in this town. Nigra children need schooling the same as our white children."

"You're right about that, Mr. Tyson. But the schools are not the same, and it's a shame!"

Mr. Tyson stood up. He looked like a giant standing beside Grandma.

Grandma went on. "Y'all's Jim Crow laws

promising equal but separate chances for colored people are hindering us from getting ahead."

Mr. Tyson opened the back door and looked around. When he returned he said, "Katie, you've got a nice place here. A yard full of plump chickens, trees loaded with oranges, and more corn and pole beans each year in your garden than I have in mine. This town has let you prosper."

Grandma offered him another piece of cake.

Mr. Tyson shook his head and said, "I'm a big heavyset white man, Katie, remember? Are you sending your young'uns to school? That's the law." Then he wrote in his little book.

Grandma put her sewing things in the basket and said, "Mr. Tyson, it's like this. The children will be going to Philadelphia soon to live with their mama and daddy. They'll go to school there."

"Woman, you are breaking the law!" He put fifty cents on the table to pay for his treats. "I'm warning you, Katie."

"In this town the colored school is too far from our homes. Our children have to walk through miles of dangerous places in the cold and rain. It's a sin and a shame."

Mr. Truant Man put his book on the table and wrote a long time. Then he said, "You are a stubborn-headed little colored woman, Katie!"

"I'm teaching them school lessons and right from wrong every day." Grandma's face was squeezed tight and her chin stuck out.

After he left the store, Grandma muttered, "When spring comes, the colored children will drop out of school to plant beans and tomatoes for the white farmers right under Tyson's nose, and he won't blink." She walked to the front and watched him speed off in his police car.

Before we ate our supper that night, Grandma made us say grace. "Say the blessing, Prince."

We bowed our heads and Prince said, "Make us true and thankful for the notions of our bodies. Amen."

Prince didn't say it right. It's "for the nourishment of our bodies."

Grandma had her mind on something and so she didn't talk 'bout Grandpa that night.

After supper she told us to get our books and study our lessons.

My school reader was the story of Baby Ray. He had fat pink cheeks and a head full of red curls. I read aloud:

> *"Baby Ray has a dog.*
> *The dog is little.*
> *Baby Ray loves the little dog.*
> *The little dog loves Baby Ray.*
>
> *Baby Ray has two kitty cats.*
> *The kitty cats are cunning.*
> *Baby Ray loves the cunning kitty cats.*
> *The cunning kitty cats love Baby Ray.*
>
> *Baby Ray lives in a large house with a*
> *porch around it.*
> *The street and sidewalk passing his*
> *house are paved and lined with tall*
> *umbrella trees making shade."*

Grandma said I was a good reader, but Prince said he could read harder stories than my Baby Ray story.

We had a bunch of books stamped with big letters that said DISCARD. Mis' Bessie brought them to us. She got them from the white children's school.

With our crayons we painted the faces of the people in the books to make them look like Grandma's patchwork quilt. We painted some faces berry black like Grandpa's. Then we made other faces brown, tan, yaller, light skinned, and pink and white, the color of Baby Ray in my easy reader.

That night, Grandma sat close to her Bible-reading table. The Bible was open, but she wasn't reading it out loud and she wasn't reading in her head. Her lips were not moving and murmuring.

Prince asked, "Grandma, is Mr. Truant Man gonna come back and make you send us to school?"

She took a long, deep breath and said, "You two children are never going to school in this town!"

"Will he put you in jail for breaking the law?"

"Prince, he won't put me in jail."

"How you know that, Grandma?"

"He's bluffing, just doing his job."

"But what if he comes and takes you to jail?"

"Don't you worry about that, child. If Mr. Tyson ever did such a thing, Reverend Hill would go straight to the courthouse and tell Judge Mel Griffin. The judge is still my friend, and he wouldn't tolerate that kind of wrongdoing. Don't ever forget that!"

Grandma closed her Bible. "It's bedtime. Say your prayers and go to sleep."

SATURDAY PAYDAY
AND MEETING TIME

Grandma's vanilla cake was in the oven. "I sure hope my customers come tonight and pay down their charges. The cake will draw them in." Grandma sometimes bragged that she was the best cake maker in town. "I use fresh eggs and pure butter. Lard is no good in cakes." The whole store, inside and outdoors, smelled like vanilla cake.

Me and Prince had gathered eggs laid by our big Rhode Island Red hens each day and Grandma put aside a dozen, one at a time, for her Saturday cake. She skimmed the cream from the milk sent over by Mis' King in exchange for groceries. When we shook the cream in a covered jar, yellow butter rose to the top. Grandma lifted the butter from the top of the jar and put it in some cold water to rinse off the curds. The leftover milk was set aside for making biscuits.

"Put more wood in the stove, Prince, so we won't freeze," said Grandma.

The cake sampler was done. Grandma always baked a little cake alongside the big one. She took it straight from the oven and cut it in two pieces for Prince and me.

"Pearl, get me a clean apron and the hair brush. I want to make myself presentable for our company tonight," Grandma said. She twisted her graying hair into a knot on top of her head.

The big cake was soft and brown and ready for Grandma to slice.

"For a dime, this is a bargain," she said.

"Pearl, you take charge of the ledger; Prince, you collect the money and put it in that cigar box."

I looked out the door to see if the people were coming out on this cold night.

"Here they come, Grandma. I see them down the road." Their shoulders were hunched and their arms were wrapped around their bodies pushing toward the store.

Saturday was payday and Sunday was resting day, so on Saturday night the store was a meeting place for laughing, joking, and arguing till everybody was ready to go home. The people were dressed in their Sunday clothes. Some of the men flashed rolls of green paper money, real money. Grandma reminded them, "Don't forget to take care of business." Grandma said the men were signifying. "They're trying to be big shots for a hot minute flashing their handfuls of greenbacks."

Bo Bringy was the first in line to take care of business.

In the ledger Grandma recorded what he paid down on his charges and what he still owed. Then she gave him change from the cigar box. Me and Prince helped.

"Careful with that money box, Prince," said Grandma. "Find the names, Pearl."

I turned the pages till I found the right name of the next person in line.

After the people finished paying down their charges, they bought candy and soda water.

"The cake is on the kitchen table," Grandma said. "Help yourself and drop a dime in the cup." Everyone rushed for the kitchen and came back to the front of the store carrying soda water and candy and stuffing their mouths with cake.

The ladies sat on the bench facing the counter. Some of the men sat on empty soda-water crates making a half circle. Grandma sat on her high stool behind the counter. You couldn't see how small she was.

They sat like a church congregation waiting for a program to begin. Grandma looked like the boss leader of the program. "I'm glad to see y'all this cold evening, for your company and your business."

Reverend Hill stood drinking a bottle of root beer as he leaned on our big green icebox.

Grandma whispered to Prince and me, "Reverend Hill is standing over there getting ready to aggravate me with his talk about a Republican Depression ruining our lives. Mr. Lincoln was a Republican; that was the party that freed the slaves."

"Mis' Katie, how are Ruth and Joe getting along in that big city?" Mis' Clara asked.

"I bet they've forgot all about us poor country folks down here," Mis' Lucille said.

"Does Ruth send you any money to help pay the children's expenses?" Mis' Ada asked.

Grandma pulled herself up and answered, "I'm satisfied. I know my children are doing the best they can. They'll write when they get around to it."

Reverend Hill stepped out and said, "Times are hard everywhere. The Republicans have ruined the whole country. Folks are standing in bread and soup lines all over the North."

The customers took sides; some on Grandma's side, the others with Reverend Hill. They talked loud and fast, and we didn't know what they were saying.

Reverend Hill leaned against the counter and said Mr. Lincoln's Republican Party was long gone. "I'm telling you to vote for Roosevelt, that new Democrat from New York. He has plans for giving all the people a chance to make a living."

"Reverend Hill reads and keeps up with all the government doings and to-do. We'd better listen to him and get wise," said Bo Bringy.

Mis' Clara said, "Pearl, get me a piece of that cake before it's all eaten up."

"It's ten cents a slice," I answered.

With her slice of cake in hand and a bottle of grape soda, Mis' Clara strutted to the center of the store and started telling about a ghost called Lentis.

"Every night when I'm on my way home from the Bronson's hot kitchen, I have to put up with Lentis. I think he can smell my pan of leftover meatloaf and mashed potatoes that I'm taking home to my young'uns.

"He rises from his grave and floats toward my face and then he circles around me. He could be trying to warn me about something. He has those same bulging eyes with bags under them. His beard is still long, white as cotton. His feet and legs are gone. When I say, 'Go back where you came from,' he floats back to the cemetery behind the church."

The people didn't move or say a word as Mis' Clara talked and circled them like the ghost man did.

Grandma said, "Poor man, after ten long years and six feet in the ground, Lentis is still trying to find peace in his soul. Before he departed from this life, he was one drinking, cussing, and fighting rascal. He couldn't hold a job, and his wife said he died hungry. She said he was always rattling pots and pans in her kitchen late at night looking for something to eat."

Me and Prince were sitting on the floor listening to Mis' Clara and Grandma tell about the ghost man. When Grandma noticed us she said, "You two should be in bed." Then she took us into her room.

"I'm scared of the ghost man, Grandma," I said.

"Nothing can hurt you here in my bed, Pearl." She covered me with her quilt and gave me a hug.

Prince didn't like for Grandma to hug him good night, so he scooted down in Grandpa's bed and pulled the cover all over himself.

Grandma turned the lamp down low and said, "Good night, sleep tight, say your prayers."

The room was dim and quiet. Not a sound came from the store. A heavy, fuzzy cloud flopped over me and squashed me down, down. I sank and landed in the ditch near the railroad trestle. Mama and Daddy reached for me, but our hands couldn't touch. I clawed the roots, pulled the bushes, and was sliding back into the ditch when I saw the ghost man bouncing up and down in front of the wardrobe in Grandma's room.

His eyes were glowing and bulging like burning charcoals. His long white beard fell to his stomach. I was sure he was Mis' Clara's ghost with no legs. My own legs locked and I couldn't move. Prince was clinging to a kite string and flying over the church and the cemetery.

"Help me, Prince! The ghost man is gonna get me."

Next thing, me and Prince filled our hands with Mama's April Showers powder and threw it at the ghost. The room sparkled with light and the ghost faded into the ceiling.

The fuzzy clouds came down on me again, and I began to fall. I held on to the quilt and called for Prince. He grabbed my shoulder and shook me real hard. "Wake up, Pearl. You're having a bad dream." I was sweating and my head was swimming. Grandma brought me water and I went back to sleep.

The next morning, Grandma woke us up early so we could take our baths and dress for Sunday school. She laid out our clean underwear and our Sunday clothes. Then she brought in the tin tubs from our wash shed and boiled water to pour in each of them to take off the chill. She gave us sweet, store-bought soap and our own set of flour sack cloths for washing and drying ourselves.

"Come on, Pearl, help me haul the buckets of water from the pump," said Prince.

We pumped and toted buckets of water for each tub. We took turns pumping and toting till each tub was half full.

"Be sure to scrub your neck and behind your ears," Grandma reminded us. When we finished bathing, Grandma rubbed Vaseline on our faces and legs to keep them from chapping.

We were always the first children to get to church because it was so close to our store. Reverend Hill let us pass out the songbooks and spread the catechism cards on the table. We read and memorized the questions and answers on the cards. "Who made you?"

"God."

"Where is God?"

"Everywhere."

When C.H., Lillie Belle, Sam, and Inez came dressed in their Sunday clothes, we looked each other up and down to see who was wearing the nicest outfit.

Reverend Hill told us to practice our song. We sang:

> *"Walk together, children,*
> *Don't you get weary.*
> *Walk together, children,*
> *Don't you get weary.*
> *There's a big camp meeting in the*
> *Promised Land."*

"Sing that last line once more, children," said Reverend Hill.

We sang at the top of our voices, " 'In the Promised La-a-a-nd.' "

Then we sat in our chairs and listened to Reverend Hill tell us 'bout the Promised Land. We didn't know much 'bout it. He said it was a beautiful place with apple trees and cherry trees blooming everlasting. All the streets and roads, he said, were paved with gold and lit up with rainbow-colored beads and ribbons. All the people had plenty of bread, honey, and milk. The people are never sad and they make a joyful noise unto the Lord.

We clapped our hands and he asked for questions.

I asked if Philadelphia and up north were in the Promised Land.

Lillie Belle frowned and rolled her eyes at me and said, "No, girl, no."

But Reverend Hill said Philadelphia and up north were promised lands in this world. The other Promised Land that we sang about was somewhere else, like Eternity, where Grandpa went to live.

I was glad that Mama and Daddy were living in a promised land in this world, but I was so tired of waiting for them to come and get us.

SPRING BRINGS

"Come look, Prince! It's springtime!"

Our orange trees were covered with sweet-smelling white blossoms. Budding honeysuckles and pink periwinkles decorated our yard and sweetened the air.

Grandma said, "What a sight you young'uns are. You're almost as tall as your grandma. Your mama and daddy won't know you!"

"Grandma, they must'a forgot we're here," I said.

"No, no. You've got it wrong. They could never forget you."

"Maybe Daddy can't find a job up north, and they'll have to come back here and live in our same house, like we did before," Prince said.

"No, Prince. Your daddy has his mind set on getting a job up north, and your mama agrees

110

with him. He's not cut out for living in this little town."

Grandma pulled the rake and hoe from under the crawl space of our house and spread packages of seeds on the ground.

"It's a fine day for planting our beets and cabbage. I'll rake the rows, and Prince can drop the seeds."

"Pearl can drop the seeds," said Prince. "I'm counting the baby chicks as they break out of their shells."

Grandma lifted her face toward the clear blue sky. She smiled and caught short breaths of air. "This is re-borning and glory time. Old Lucifer has lost his stranglehold! Mother Earth is springing back to life," she said.

It was still spring when Daddy's letter came. Grandma read it to us:

"Ruth is expecting soon. I'm coming to get Pearl and Prince. We want them to be here before the new baby comes. I have a steady-income job as a Pullman porter on a train running between Philadelphia and Chicago. The pay with the tips is enough to live on.

I've paid back the money we borrowed from the bank to come up here. The enclosed is for your trouble.

Pearl and Prince can go to a school up here close to where we live, and they'll be good company for Ruth since I'll be on the road a lot. We thank you for all you've done for us.

Yours Truly,
Joe"

Grandma put the "enclosed" in her pocketbook and said, "This money can help me restock my empty shelves and keep my credit and name in good standing."

"Read it again, Grandma!" I said.

"Show me the letter, Grandma," said Prince.

We spread the letter on the table and looked at it a long time. We recognized the long word "Philadelphia" followed by "PA."

"What's 'PA,' Grandma?"

Grandma said it was a short word for Pennsylvania. She wrote "Pennsylvania" on Daddy's letter and we said it over and over again.

"Pennsylvania, Pennsylvania!"

"Is Pennsylvania in Philadelphia?" I asked.

Grandma phewed and said, "When you get to Philadelphia, ask your mama and daddy to buy a geography book for you." Then Grandma drew a picture of Pennsylvania that looked like a hen's nest full of different sizes of eggs.

"The largest egg stands for Philadelphia," she said.

After reading Daddy's letter, we didn't know what to do with ourselves. We chased each other over to our house and back to the store again, just like we used to play before Daddy and Mama left to go up north.

Grandma told us to calm down and help her get our house cleaned up for Daddy.

The days crawled by like stuck-in-the-mud birthdays!

"When is Daddy gonna get here? How much longer before he gets here?" I kept asking Grandma.

At the end of the week Prince said, "Daddy's not coming. He changed his mind."

"Prince, you don't know what you're talking 'bout." I made an ugly face at him.

"When is Daddy coming for us, Grandma?" I asked.

"Soon. Before you can say 'Mollie Whuppie found her puppy.' "

Grandma kept busy washing, ironing, and sewing our clothes.

"Take care of the store while I make your clothes look tidy and clean. Can't let you leave me in rags and tatters," Grandma said.

She soaped and boiled piles of used flour sacks until they were snow white and fluffy soft. Then she pulled the ripping threads from each sack and ironed and stitched them into wide sheets. All the while she hummed her favorite hymn, "Lead Kindly Light." With her pile of sheets she cut out and made bloomers and petticoats for me, drawers and undershirts for Prince, and little sack coats with yellow ribbon ties. They were baby kimonos for the baby that was coming.

"You young'uns are gonna need a lot of clothes in that cold climate up north."

For the hundredth time I asked Grandma when Daddy was coming to get us.

Grandma said, "Soon. Before you can say 'Peas puddin' hot.' He's coming when he gets time off from his new Pullman porter job. Hold your horses. He'll be here for sure."

We gave up our road watching and returned to the store.

"Keep your mind on your work, and the time for your daddy to get here will come quicker," Grandma said.

Every time a customer stopped to rest or buy stuff, we blurted out that Daddy was coming to take us up north to live with him and Mama.

We told Mis' Lucille and she said, "Yeah, yeah. He's coming." I could tell she didn't believe me.

The day he came, we had our minds on our work. We checked on the mousetraps placed around the burlap bags of onions and potatoes. A trap snapped. A fat mouse squeaked.

Prince said, "We've got one!"

We took it outside to bury it. We called out to Grandma, "We caught another mouse!"

Grandma said the mice and her nonpaying customers were going to put her out of business. We were washing traps and putting in

bits of cheese when Daddy sneaked up behind us.

He called our names just like he used to: "Hey, Pearl! Hey, Prince!"

I couldn't speak or move. Prince couldn't either.

"What's wrong? The cat's got your tongues?"

My tongue was tied tight.

He lifted Prince and then me. "You are too heavy for your daddy."

For the longest time we didn't say a word. We just stared at Daddy.

He was bigger than he used to be.

I asked, "Are you Daddy?"

He was not wearing overalls or that blue serge monkey suit that he didn't like wearing.

His shirt and pants were the same color of brown.

Grandma rushed outdoors to see Daddy and hugged him. She pulled him back and forth and said, "I'm glad you're back home. We've been waiting for you."

We stood away from Daddy and looked him all over.

He threw his suitcase on the porch and took our hands. He turned us around and asked, "What's your grandma been feeding you? Collard greens and corn pone?"

"Get your pa a cold soda, Prince," said Grandma.

"Why didn't Mama come with you, Daddy?" I asked.

"Well, your mama is very busy getting ready for you and Prince to live with us."

For supper Grandma baked a chicken and made a skillet of corn pudding.

Daddy ate a big dinner and tried to get us talking. "What is percolating in those heads of yours?" he asked.

Our daddy was real, and I could not think what to say!

Then Prince started asking one question after another. "Where do you sleep on the train, Daddy? When are we going to ride on the train? Where do you go to the toilet?"

"There are no outhouses on the train. The toilets are the same as the ones at the depot with tanks of running water above the seat," Daddy said.

"Are we always gonna live up north?" I asked.

"Now you young'uns are full of questions," Daddy said.

Grandma was quiet. "Let your daddy get a little rest."

Before Daddy came, Grandma had put starched white curtains on the windows and a crocheted counterpane on the bed. Daddy was going to sleep in the bedroom that was Mama's before she married Daddy. A picture of Mama was on the dresser.

"Can I sleep with you, Daddy?" asked Prince.

"Can I sleep with you, too, Daddy?" I asked.

That night, we followed Daddy every-where—step for step to the pump to get fresh water, to the porch in front of the store where he chewed tobacco, and even to the outhouse, where we waited for him to come out.

Grandma shook her head and said, "Your daddy can't move without you two on his heels!"

As we crowded into bed with Daddy, he took Mama's picture from the dresser and started imitating her. "I wonder what my children are doing right this minute? I wonder what Daddy, Prince, and Pearl are talking 'bout, right now?"

Then he put the picture back, and before we could say "I see the moon," Daddy was snoring.

The next morning I woke up in Grandma's bed and Prince was sleeping in Grandpa's bed.

Grandma was folding and packing all those clean new clothes for me and Prince, and for that baby we were getting. "Your grandpa's old humpback trunk is just right for your things," she said.

While Grandma made a picnic basket of fried chicken, cupcakes, and apples for us to eat on the train, Daddy and Prince mended the fence around Grandma's kitchen garden to keep out the raccoons and rabbits.

I tended the store by myself. I bounced up and down and sang,

> *"Now Mis' Sally,*
> *Won't you jump for joy?*
> *Jump! Jump! Jump!"*

LEAVING GRANDMA

Reverend Hill drove us to the train depot in his Ford. "I'll pick you up on my way home from the post office, Mis' Katie."

Grandma and Daddy stood close as they whispered 'bout Mama.

"Tell her to rub lard over her belly every night."

Daddy nodded and smiled. Grandma looked so small standing beside Daddy. She was not much taller than Prince.

She walked over to the water fountain to get a sip of water for washing down a Stanback headache powder.

Me and Prince had our hands locked in Daddy's. We pulled and swung around him, shoved each other, and giggled with Daddy. We could not stop giggling.

Grandma stayed at the water fountain by herself.

Daddy said, "Let's go and talk with your grandma."

A sad feeling rushed up inside of me. I dropped Daddy's hand and ran over to Grandma. I wrapped my arms around her waist.

"Come with us, please, Grandma," I begged.

Prince came over, too, and said, "Yeah, Grandma, come on. You can make a store in Philadelphia."

Grandma chuckled and said, "You two young'uns are a mess. Your mama and daddy don't have room enough for me."

"You can have my room," Prince offered.

"It's time for you to leave me and live with your daddy and mama. It's time for me to tend to my business right here. Thank you for the invitation."

Daddy's arm was on Grandma's shoulder. He said, "Mama Katie, our home is always open to you."

Grandma folded her arms around us and said, "You children need to go to school and get book learning. You need friends your own age.

When school is out in the summertime, come on back here to help me run the store."

Reverend Hill returned with a sack of roasted peanuts and a cloth bag of books and comics for us to have on the train. The books and comics were our favorites. Daddy liked them, too. We sat on the bench in the waiting room and looked at the pictures and listened to Reverend Hill read the story about the fox and the sour grapes. It was from the book of Aesop's fables.

The fox kept jumping up and down trying to get the juicy grapes hanging on the vine. He couldn't jump high enough to reach the grapes, so he pretended that they were sour and he didn't want them.

After a while the giant train rumbled in. The conductor called out, "All aboard!"

Daddy lifted me, and the conductor helped Prince climb the tall steps leading to our car.

Daddy pointed to double seats next to the window and we sat looking out and waving until the depot was out of sight and we couldn't see Grandma anymore. The train rumbled on and on into the dark night. We leaned on

Daddy and fell asleep. When we woke up, we ate peanuts and apples, walked through the aisle, looked at the sleepy faces of the people, and went to the toilet. I was already tired of the long train ride.

It took two nights and one and a half days. We kept asking Daddy, "When do we get there?"

Daddy told us to look out the window as he pointed to places we didn't know about. The train rolled through tunnels, over bridges, up mountains, and through little towns in valleys. All the time I missed Grandma and pictured her standing with Reverend Hill at the depot. Her voice kept ringing in my ears. "These folk must think my store is Noah's Ark and I'm Mis' Noah."

"How much longer, Daddy?" I asked. My stomach ached.

"Read your books and your comics," said Daddy.

I didn't want to read 'cause I was thinking 'bout lots of things. "Prince, does Grandma think we don't love her anymore?"

"Pearl, I love her a lot. Maybe Mama can tell her to come to Philadelphia."

I wished I was two Pearls—one for Mama and one for Grandma.

We leaned on Daddy's outstretched arms.

"When the baby comes, your grandma will come visit us, I'll betcha. And when this train pulls into that Union Railroad station, you're gonna see your happy mama waiting for you," he promised.

"Daddy, is Mama getting a baby 'cause she left us with Grandma?"

Daddy closed his eyes and said, "Uhmmmm."

"Talk, Daddy," I said.

"Yep. You and Prince stayed on her mind all the time. Pearl this. Prince that. We talked about you day in and day out."

We slept some more for a long time. We were awakened by the conductor calling, "Washington, D.C."

Prince shook me and repeated, "Washington, D.C.! Washington, D.C.!"

I was not sleepy anymore.

"Are we up north?" asked Prince.

"Pretty close," said Daddy.

Some people got up and left the train. Then the train started moving again, and after a short time the conductor called, "Baltimore, Maryland." We bounced back and forth on our seats.

Daddy said, "Hold your horses!"

We were about to pop open, but before we could say "Peas puddin' hot," the conductor called, "Wilmington, Delaware," just like Grandma said.

Lots of people got off the train at each station the conductor called. Most of the colored people stayed on. The men talked loud 'bout crossing the Mason-Dixon Line. Suddenly they leaped from their seats and shouted, "This is the Promised Land! This is the Promised Land!"

"We've crossed over!" Daddy clapped his hands and pulled us close to him.

"This is the land of the free, children. We're nearing the City of Brotherly Love! Gather your belongings and tie your shoelaces!"

He pulled our bags down from the overhead rack and helped us get into our coats. With his hand he smoothed my braids.

"Tuck your shirt in, Prince. We're almost

home, children. The next call the conductor is gonna make is Philadelphia, Pennsylvania!"

"Mama is waiting for us," I said out loud.

"Hold on to me, children. Don't let go." With bags in each hand, Daddy shoved us through the train aisle.

The train clanked to a stop, and we hopped down onto the landing place. It was crowded with people. We couldn't see around the wall of tall moving legs. We gripped the handles of Daddy's suitcase. I held on to the bag of books, and Prince carried the rest of the peanuts, the pencils, and Mama's slate.

We climbed lots of steep stairs leading to a sky-high room. It had floor-to-ceiling windows all around and pictures up above. The room was like a world all lit up, finer than our post office, bank, courthouse, drugstore, and depot all put together! There were hundreds of people moving about, and some sitting on long shiny benches with high backs.

"Don't stumble and fall. You'll get trampled," Daddy warned.

We kept looking, but we didn't see Mama. "Where is Mama, Daddy?"

He pointed to a bench. "There she is. Waiting for us."

At first, I didn't know who she was. She just looked like a lady wearing a dark coat, sitting alone on the bench. Then she saw us and called our names. "Prince! Pearl!"

Her face was round and soft, but she looked swollen, like she had swallowed a pumpkin.

I yelled, "Mama, Mama!" and ran into her outstretched arms.

Prince fell into her arms, too, and Mama held us both. She hugged and kissed us and looked us over. "Oh, how you young'uns have grown!"

She smelled like April Showers talcum powder.

"Mama, are you gonna keep us with you always?"

"Yes, yes, we're going to take care of you always!"

"Mama, do you like living up north more than you liked living in our house next door to Grandma's store?"

Questions tumbled from our mouths.

"Are you getting a baby because you didn't have us with you?"

"Mama, did you worry 'cause we were so mad when you and Daddy didn't buy a ticket for us to ride on the train with you?"

"Every minute of the day I ached to see you and Prince," said Mama.

Daddy was sitting on the bench next to Mama. His face was bright and smiling. "Good times ahead, children!"

"Mama, I'm gonna be a rule maker after I get a lot of book learning!" said Prince.

"I'm gonna get a lot of book learning and be a rule maker, too, Mama!"

"Well, bless my soul. What kind of rules are you two planning on making?"

"Grandma said rule makers can make new rules to 'low colored children to use libraries and attend schools with sidewalks."

Mama laughed and said, "Joe, do you hear these young'uns talking just like Mama?"

"We're up north. This is Quaker county! Ben Franklin's town. The Quakers and old Ben were right-thinking people! And the rule makers listened to them! Every child here can attend schools with sidewalks!" said Daddy.

"You don't have to walk through those fields and along those dangerous highways to get

a little book learning anymore," said Mama.

Daddy checked his watch and said he was going to see about the rest of our luggage. "I'll have them sent out. Ruth, your mama has sent your daddy's humpback trunk crammed with clothes for the young'uns."

While we waited for Daddy, Mama kept telling us to stand up, turn around, sit beside her, and stand up again so she could look at us. She was the same way she used to be before she left us with Grandma.

When Daddy came back, he helped us collect our hand-carried bags. "Let's go home, family."

Mama pulled herself from the bench and rubbed her back. "We'll take the streetcar."

A little train stopped in front of the big depot. The driver opened the door and let us on. We sat in the front seats. Daddy paid the driver and sat with Prince. The little train was soon filled with white people and colored people sitting and standing side by side. It jangled past crowds of hurrying people and tall buildings pushing through the sky. A banging, clanking, zooming commotion filled the air.

GRANDMA'S GENERAL STORE
THE ARK

"Race you, Pearl. The last one to Grandma's is a rotten egg," Prince dared me.

"The first one there is a polecat," I came back at him. I could run as fast as Prince, though he was almost seven and I was still five.

We raced to the store, just next door to the house where me and Prince lived with Mama and Daddy. Me and Prince had two homes where we played, ate, and slept whenever we wanted.

Grandma called the store an "add-on." Grandpa built it onto their ready-made house. "It's my Ark," she said.

"What's an Ark?" I asked.

Grandma paused a long while before she answered. "A shelter from the storms of life. It keeps you from being tossed away."

"Grandma, are you scared of storms?"

"No, child. Only the ones I don't expect. They make a heap of trouble and pain." Grandma talked riddles at times.

The store sat on a ridge above the railroad tracks. Every day we waved at the train chugging along, blowing its whistle and spitting out steam. It smelled hot and smoky. "Stay away from that railroad crossing," Grandma warned.

Watching the colored customers and white merchants straggle into the store was our favorite thing to do. They talked a lot and we listened. Grandma was always saying, "They're just here to palaver."

When I asked her what "palaver" meant, she said, "Business is slow for the merchants, and my customers don't have much money to spend. They're just here waiting around and treating themselves to a cold soda and a sweet snack to help pass the time of day. We laugh and talk together."

The customers squeezed together on a bench facing the counter where Grandma kept the scales and charging ledger. A framed picture